CCER
3 ·'02

W9-COO-461

Silly Questions

Written by Lynea Bowdish
Illustrated by Eldon C. Doty

Children's Press®
A Division of Scholastic Inc.
New York • Toronto • London • Auckland • Sydney
Mexico City • New Delhi • Hong Kong
Danbury, Connecticut

For Lois Carlsten Smith, loving cousin
and supportive friend, to add to her collection.
—L. B.

To Sally Doty
—E. C. D.

Reading Consultant
Katharine A. Kane
Education Consultant
(Retired, San Diego County Office of Education
and San Diego State University)

Visit Children's Press® on the Internet at:
http://publishing.grolier.com

Library of Congress Cataloging-in-Publication Data
Bowdish, Lynea.
  Silly questions / written by Lynea Bowdish ; illustrated by Eldon
C. Doty.
  p. cm. — (Rookie reader)
  Summary: Asks such outrageous questions as "Have you ever
tried making an elephant laugh?" "Have you waltzed with a penguin?"
and "Have you sung a duet with a curly-haired moose?"
  ISBN 0-516-22230-9 (lib. bdg.)   0-516-25972-5 (pbk.)
  [1. Animals—Fiction. 2. Stories in rhyme.] I. Doty, Eldon, ill. II.
Title. III. Series.
PZ8.3.B6725 Si 2001
[E]—dc21   00-047377

GROLIER
PUBLISHING 1 2 3 4 5 6 7 8 9 10 R 10 09 08 07 06 05 04 03 02 01

Have you ever tried making
an elephant laugh,

or tickled a turtle,

or kissed a giraffe?

Have you waltzed with a penguin,

9

or dined with a bat,

or fished with a frog
in a big yellow hat?

13

14

Maybe you've tried shaking
hands with a snake,

15

or helped a pink octopus
eat birthday cake.

17

Have you sung a duet with
a curly-haired moose,

19

or hugged a gorilla,

or bowled with a goose?

Have you bathed
with a walrus,

or read to a fly?

You haven't?

29

Well truthfully, neither have I.

Word List (57 words)

a	elephant	haven't	or	truthfully
an	ever	helped	penguin	turtle
bat	fished	hugged	pink	walrus
bathed	fly	I	questions	waltzed
big	frog	in	read	well
birthday	giraffe	kissed	shaking	with
bowled	goose	laugh	silly	yellow
cake	gorilla	making	snake	you
curly	haired	maybe	sung	you've
dined	hands	moose	tickled	
duet	hat	neither	to	
eat	have	octopus	tried	

About the Author

Lynea Bowdish lives in Hollywood, Maryland, with her husban David Roberts, two dogs, one goldfish, and one pink plastic flaming She likes bird and butterfly watching, and sometimes tries to gro flowers. She often asks herself, and others, silly questions.

About the Illustrator

At fifty-seven years of age, Eldon Doty lives with his wife and litt dog, Soupy, in Santa Rosa, California. He learned to draw as a k copying magazines. He later graduated from the University Washington with a degree in history. After serving as a policeman f thirteen years, he attended the Academy of Art in San Francisco the early 1980s. He has illustrated a number of children's books well as created humorous illustrations for advertisements, scho textbooks, and corporate publications. His favorite drawing in th book is the curly-haired moose.